For Meghan—you are an amazing, creative spirit

LOUISE

Modern
Movers

SOLD

Rothko Realty
expressive home sales
555-0631

AND

Andie

THE ART OF FRIENDSHIP

KELLY LIGHT

BALZER+BRAY
AN IMPRINT OF HARPERCOLLINS*PUBLISHERS*

Art, this is the BEST day ever!
I'm so excited to meet our new neighbor.
I hope she loves art too.

Hi, I'm Louise.
This is Art . . . and our cat.

I'm Andie. This is Bacon. Come in.

I just knew we'd have
so much in common.

Do you want to draw together?

This is the . . .

What do you think?

Hmm, needs something here. . . .

I think it looks fine.

Let me—

No!

I think we have
artistic differences.

It was nice to meet you.

Oh, Bacon.
How can I fix this?

This is the worst day ever.

Look what we made together.

It's perfect.

I know what our next art project is going to be. . . .

Balzer + Bray is an imprint of HarperCollins Publishers.

Louise and Andie: The Art of Friendship
Copyright © 2016 by Kelly Light
All rights reserved. Manufactured in China.
No part of this book may be used or reproduced in any manner whatsoever without written
permission except in the case of brief quotations embodied in critical articles and reviews.
For information address HarperCollins Children's Books, a division of HarperCollins Publishers,
195 Broadway, New York, NY 10007.
www.harpercollinschildrens.com

ISBN 978-0-06-234440-3 (trade bdg.)

The artist used many black Prismacolor pencils
and Photoshop to create the illustrations for this book.
Typography by Alison Donalty
16 17 18 19 20   SCP   10 9 8 7 6 5 4 3 2 1
❖ First Edition